SADDLEBACK *Classics*

KIDNAPPED

ROBERT LOUIS STEVENSON

ADAPTED BY

Janice Greene

SADDLEBACK
PUBLISHING·INC.

SADDLEBACK *Classics*

Development and Production: Laurel Associates, Inc.
Cover and Interior Art: Black Eagle Productions

SADDLEBACK
PUBLISHING·INC.
Three Watson
Irvine, CA 92618-2767
Website: www.sdlback.com

ISBN 1-56254-873-5

Printed in the United States of America
11 10 09 08 07 06   9 8 7 6 5 4 3 2 1

CONTENTS

1 The Mysterious House of Shaws

In June of 1751, I locked the door of my father's house for the last time.

As I walked down the road, I came upon Mr. Campbell. This kind man was the minister in our little town, Essendean. "Are you sorry to leave home, boy?" he asked kindly.

"I've been happy here," I said. "But since my father and mother are both dead, there's no reason to stay. To speak the truth, I do not know where I am going."

"Very well, Davie," Mr. Campbell replied. "I have a letter to give you. Your father wrote it when he knew he was dying. It is your inheritance. He said you are to take this letter to the house of Shaws."

"The house of Shaws!" I cried out. "What did a poor man like my father have to do with the house of Shaws?"

"Who can say for sure?" Mr. Campbell

said. "But that is your name, Davie—Balfour of Shaws."

Then he handed me the envelope. The words on it said: *For Ebenezer Balfour of Shaws, to be delivered by my son, David Balfour.* My heart beat hard. This was a great prospect for a poor boy of 17.

The house of Shaws was a two-day walk. It was in the neighborhood of Cramond, near the great city of Edinburgh. Mr. Campbell gave me some advice as we walked along. He said I should be quick to understand things, but slow to speak. He added that I must obey the master of the house of Shaws. I promised to do my best.

Mr. Campbell spoke comforting words. He promised that if my rich relatives turned me away, I could always stay with him.

Before he turned back, he gave me four things. The first was a little money from the sale of my father's belongings. Then there were three gifts from him and his wife: a coin, a bible, and instructions for making Lily of the Valley water. He explained that this water is good for the body in health and in sickness.

On the second day of my journey, I came up a hill. Just below me was the city of Edinburgh, smoking like an oven. I saw a flag on the Edinburgh castle and ships in the water nearby. The sight of the busy, crowded city brought my heart to my mouth.

Soon I reached the neighborhood of Cramond. I began to ask directions to the house of Shaws. The question seemed to surprise people. One man frowned and said, "If you'll take a word from me, you'll keep clear of the house of Shaws."

I came across a barber. Knowing that barbers are great gossips, I asked him, "What sort of man is Ebenezer Balfour?"

"Why, he's no sort of man," the barber grumbled. "No sort of man at all!"

If I wasn't so far from home, I would have turned back. But I was a bit tired after coming all this way. I wanted to see the house of Shaws for myself.

Near sundown I met a dark, sour-looking woman. Again, I asked the way to the house of Shaws. She pointed to a great, dark bulk of a building. The place looked like a ruin.

"That?" I said.

The woman's face grew angry and bitter. "Blood built that place!" she cried. "And blood shall bring it down! When you see the master, tell him Jennet Clouston has put a curse on his house! Black be their fall!"

Then she left me. Her words had sapped the energy from my legs. I sat down and stared at the house until the sun went down. Then I saw smoke rising from the chimney. That meant fire, and warmth, and people inside. It comforted my heart wonderfully.

As I walked up to the door, I saw that part of the building had never been finished. Some rooms and a stairway were open to the sky! Bats flew in and out of several windows that had no glass.

Was *this* the house of Shaws? I had imagined a palace. I had hoped to find friends and perhaps a fortune within these walls.

Inside, I heard dishes rattling, and a dry cough. But when I knocked on the door, the house became dead silent. All I could hear was a clock ticking inside. Whoever was in the house must have been listening, too.

I felt like running away. Then a flash of anger got the upper hand. I pounded on the door and shouted for Mr. Balfour.

I heard the cough overhead. When I looked up, I saw a man's head and the wide-muzzle end of a blunderbuss—aimed at me!

"It's loaded," his stern voice snarled.

"I've come with a letter," I explained. "Is Mr. Ebenezer Balfour of Shaws here?"

"You can put the letter on the doorstep and be off," the man said.

"I will do no such thing," I said. "I have a

letter of introduction for Mr. Balfour."

There was a long pause. Then the man said, "Who are you?"

"I'm not ashamed of my name," I said. "I am David Balfour."

The man seemed to be startled, because I heard the blunderbuss rattling on the windowsill. After a very long pause, he said, "Your father must be dead. That's what brings you knocking at my door. All right, then. I'll let you in," he went on defiantly. With that, he disappeared from the window.

There was a great rattling of chains and bolts. Then the door was opened—and quickly shut again as I stepped inside.

"Go into the kitchen and touch nothing," the grizzled old man said with a grunt.

I groped my way forward in the dark. The bright fire in the kitchen lit up the barest room I'd ever seen. Half a dozen dishes stood on the shelves. The table was set for supper. I saw a bowl of porridge, a spoon, and a cup of beer. Padlocks hung from chests along the wall and a corner cupboard.

The man was stooped, narrow-shouldered,

and unshaven. Above his ragged shirt, his face was the color of clay. His age could have been either 50 or 70. What bothered me most were his eyes. He never stopped watching me—but he refused to look me square in the face. I couldn't tell what sort of man he was. To me, he looked like an old servant, left behind, perhaps, to watch the place.

"Let's see the letter," he demanded.

I told him the letter was for Mr. Balfour, not for him.

"And who do you think *I* am?" he asked. "Give me Alexander's letter!"

"You know my father's name?" I gasped.

"It would be strange if I didn't," he said. "He was my own brother! And though you don't seem to like me much, I'm your uncle. So sit down, Davie. Have some porridge, and let me see that letter."

What a rude man! If I'd been younger, I would have burst into tears from the disappointment. Finding no words to say, I sat down. But I had no appetite at all.

My uncle stooped over the fire, turning the letter over in his hands. "Don't you know what's in the letter, young man?" he asked.

"You can see for yourself, sir," I replied. "The seal has not been broken."

"I see," he said, "but tell me, what brought you here?"

"Why, to give you the letter," I said.

"But you had some hopes, no doubt?" His face took on a cunning look.

"I confess, sir," I stammered, "that it lifted my spirits to hear that I had well-to-do family. I hoped they might help me in life. But I'm no beggar, sir. I want no favors unless they're freely given. As poor as I seem, I have friends of my own who will help me."

"Hoot-toot!" Uncle Ebenezer said. "Don't get upset with me. We'll get along fine."

I watched him as he ate his porridge. He kept darting glances at my old shoes and my homespun stockings. Once, though, our eyes met accidentally. He looked like a thief who'd been caught with his hand in a man's pocket!

After a while, he asked sharply, "Has your father been dead long?"

"Three weeks, sir," I said.

"Has he never mentioned me?" he asked.

"I never knew that he had a brother until you told me," I replied. For some reason my answer seemed to improve his mood. Then he announced that it was time for bed.

He lit no lamp or candle, but groped his way out of the dark kitchen. I followed him to an upstairs room and asked for a light.

"Hoot-toot!" he said. "I don't agree with lights in the house—I'm afraid of fires, you see. Good night to you, Davie, my man." He closed the door and locked me inside.

The fine, embroidered furniture in the room was rotting from years of disuse. The bed was cold and damp. I pulled a blanket out of my backpack and slept on the floor.

The next morning, I banged on the door until he let me out. My breakfast was porridge and beer again.

"Davie," the old man said, "you've done well to come to your Uncle Ebenezer. I mean to do right by you. Meanwhile, just give me a day or two to make a plan. And don't say anything to anybody."

With that, he took an old coat and hat from the cupboard. Locking it behind him, he said he was going out. "I can't leave you by yourself in the house," he added. "I'm afraid I'll have to lock you out."

Blood rushed to my face as I took in the insult. "If you lock me out," I said, "that's the last you'll see of me as a friend."

He turned away, trembling, twitching, and mumbling to himself. But when he looked back at me, he had a smile on his face.

"Uncle Ebenezer," I said, "I can make no sense of this. You treat me like a thief. You don't trust me in your house. It's not possible that you can really accept me. Let me go back to my own good friends at home!"

"No, no!" he said very earnestly. "I do accept you, Davie. We'll get along yet. For the honor of the house, I can't let you leave the way you came. Stay a while—there's a good boy—and you'll find we'll come to an understanding."

I was silent for a time. Then I said, "All right, sir, I'll stay—but only for a while. If we don't get along, it will be no fault of mine."

 # 2 My Uncle's Betrayal

Before leaving, my uncle showed me to a room next to the kitchen. It was full of books, both in Latin and English. I took pleasure in reading until my uncle returned.

In one book I had found something quite strange. The inscription read as follows: *To my brother Ebenezer, on his fifth birthday.* The handwriting was excellent.

I'd assumed that my father was the younger brother. How, then, could he write so well when he was not yet five years old?

Then an idea occurred to me: I asked my uncle if he and my father had been twins.

The question made him jump. "Why do you ask that?" he demanded. He grabbed hold of the front of my jacket. His eyes were blinking strangely.

"Take your hand off my jacket," I said calmly. I was far stronger than he, and was not easily frightened by his rough ways.

"Don't speak to me about your father," he said. He was shaking.

Now I began to wonder if my uncle might be insane. An old song also came to me. It was about a relative cheating a poor boy out of his inheritance.

I began to watch him as he watched me. Now we were like cat and mouse.

After a while, he asked me to bring him a chest from upstairs. "You can only reach it from the outside," he said, "in the part of the house that is not finished."

"May I have a light, sir?" I asked.

"No," he said. "I told you—no lights in my house."

"Very well," I said. "Are the stairs sound?"

"Oh, yes, they're grand," he said.

Out I went into the night. I heard the wind moaning as I unlocked the door to the stairs. Suddenly, without any warning of thunder, the whole sky lit up and then quickly went black again.

Once inside the tower, I began to feel my way up the stairs. The house of Shaws was five stories high. As I went up, another blink of summer lightning came and went. Fear caught me by the throat. I noticed that the steps were of unequal length. One of my feet was just two inches from the open stairwell!

This was the "grand" stair? A kind of angry courage flooded my heart. I crawled forward, feeling every inch before me. Bats from the tower beat against my face and body. Then, as I rounded a turn in the tower, I slipped on the edge of a step. Beyond this step was nothing but empty air! The stairs went no higher. To send a stranger up these stairs was to send him to his death. When I thought of how far I might have fallen, I broke out in a sweat.

As I groped my way downstairs again, the rain was falling in buckets. I walked softly to the kitchen and peeked inside.

My uncle sat at the table with his back to me. A bottle of spirits stood before him. He was shuddering and groaning as he drank.

After silently creeping up from behind, I clapped my hands down on his shoulders and cried out, "Ah!"

My uncle gave a broken cry and tumbled

to the floor. He lay there like a dead man. This shocked me some, but I let him lie there.

I took his keys and looked inside the cupboard. Nothing was there but bills and papers. Then I unlocked the chests. There I found money bags, more papers, and a rusty, old dagger. After hiding the dagger in my coat, I turned to my uncle.

"Come, come, man," I said. "Sit up."

"Are you alive?" he sobbed. He looked at me and shuddered in terror.

"I am," I said, "small thanks to you."

He seemed to have trouble breathing. I felt pity for him—but I was also full of anger. I told him there were several things he must explain: Why had he lied to me with every word? Why did he seem to be afraid I would leave? And why had he tried to kill me?

In a broken voice, he begged me to let him go to bed. "I'll tell you in the morning," he promised, "—as sure as death I will."

He was so weak, I had to agree. I locked him in his room and went to sleep.

The next morning, my uncle promised that he'd talk with me after breakfast. But we were interrupted by a knock at the door. It was a half-grown boy in sailor's clothes. He'd come to deliver a letter to my uncle. The boy's face was blue with cold. When he said he was hungry, I invited him in to eat the remains of my breakfast.

Uncle Ebenezer read the letter and showed it to me. It was from a man named Hoseason.

"You see, Davie," my uncle said, "I have some business to do with this man, Hoseason. He is the captain of a trading ship, the *Covenant*. It's docked at Queensferry. Come there with me, for there are papers I must sign. We can also call on the lawyer, Mr. Rankeillor, and talk about your future. You may not believe me, but you'll believe Mr. Rankeillor. He's a highly respected man—and he liked your father."

"Very well," I said. "Let us go."

My uncle said nothing as we walked along, so I spoke with the boy. He told me his name was Ransome, and that he was the cabin boy on the *Covenant*. He described the captain as a fierce, brutal man, but it was clear Ransome admired him. He said the captain had one flaw. "He ain't no seaman," Ransome said. "It's Mr. Shuan that navigates the ship. He's the finest seaman there is—except when he's drinking. Just look here."

He pulled down his stocking and showed me a great, raw, red wound. "Mr. Shuan done that," he said, proudly.

"What!" I cried. "And you allow him to treat you so cruelly?"

The poor boy immediately changed his tune. "No!" he cried. "And just let him try!" Then he swore a silly, meaningless oath.

I have never felt such pity for anyone as I felt for that poor half-witted boy. The *Covenant* sounded like a hell on the seas.

Upon reaching Queensferry, we went to an upstairs room at an inn. There we met Captain Hoseason, a tall, dark, sober-looking man. My uncle told me to wait outside while they talked.

I was glad. Heated by a great coal fire, the captain's room was terribly hot. So I was fool enough to leave my uncle alone.

Ransome and I went downstairs to the inn's small dining room. While we ate and drank, I watched the landlord. He seemed an honest enough fellow, so I asked him if he knew a lawyer named Rankeillor.

The landlord nodded his head. "Oh, yes," he said. "He's a very honest man. And was that you who came with Ebenezer? Are you a relative? You look a bit like Mr. Alexander, Ebenezer's brother."

My father! I quickly told him that I was no relative of Ebenezer's. Then I asked if Ebenezer was well-liked in town.

"Oh, no!" the landlord exclaimed. "He's a wicked old man. There's Jennet Clouston and many other people he's driven out of house and home. And, of course, there's also talk of what he did to Mr. Alexander."

"What was that?" I asked.

"Oh, just that he killed him," said the landlord. "Surely you've heard that."

"Why would he do that?" I asked.

"To get his hands on the Shaws, of course," the landlord said.

I was shocked. "Is that so?" I said. "Was my—was Alexander the eldest son?"

"Indeed he was," the landlord replied.

"Why else would Ebenezer have killed him?"

Of course, I had guessed it before. But it is one thing to guess, and another to know. I sat stunned. I could hardly believe that I was the rightful heir to a house and land.

Captain Hoseason and my uncle met us in the street. "Davie," the captain said, "Mr. Balfour has been telling me great things about you. And for my own part, I like your looks. You shall come on board my ship and drink a bowl with me."

I longed to see the inside of a ship. But I was fearful of putting myself in jeopardy. I told him that my uncle and I had an appointment with a lawyer.

"Yes, yes," he said. "Your uncle told me that. But the boat will set you ashore on the pier. And that's close to Rankeillor's house."

Then without warning, he suddenly leaned down and whispered, "Watch out for the old man. He means mischief. Come on board until I can have a word with you." With that, he slipped his arm through mine and started leading me toward the boat.

I didn't dream of hanging back. I thought

(poor fool!) that I had found a new friend!

As soon as we stepped on board, the *Covenant* began to move. The captain pointed out various parts of the ship. I was awed by the strange new sights.

Then a strange feeling came over me. "But where is my uncle?" I asked.

Hoseason's face suddenly turned grim. "Yes," he said sourly, "that's the point."

In a fit of panic, I ran to the end of the deck. There I saw my uncle in a small boat headed for shore. "Help! Help! *Murder!*" I cried. My uncle turned around, showing me a face full of cruelty and terror.

That was the last I saw of him. Strong hands took hold of me, pulling me from the side of the ship. Then a great thunderbolt seemed to strike me. I saw a bright flash of something like fire before I fell, senseless.

 **Aboard the Covenant**

When I came to, I was bound hand and foot and in great pain. Because it was so dark, I knew I must be in the bottom of the ship. Besides the aching wound on my head, I was terribly seasick.

After some time, a small man of about 30 appeared with a lantern. He washed and bandaged my wound. Then he asked if I wanted to eat, but I could not.

The next day, the little man brought Captain Hoseason to see me. "Now, sir," he said to the captain, "the boy has a high fever and no appetite. You know what that means. I want him moved to the forecastle."

But Captain Hoseason shook his head impatiently. "No, Mr. Riach, the boy is here and here he will stay."

"As second officer of this old tub," the small man said, "I demand to know if you've been paid by the uncle to do murder—"

"What kind of talk is that!" Captain Hoseason cried. "If you say the lad will die—"

"He *will!*" Mr. Riach said.

"Well, then, move him where you please!" the captain said angrily.

Five minutes later, my bonds were cut, and I was carried to the forecastle. For many days, I lay there listening to the sailors talking. They were a rough lot. Some of them had been pirates, and some had done things it would shame me even to mention.

Yet they were not all bad. For one thing, they returned the money I'd had in my pocket. It was about a third short, but I was very glad to get it. I hoped it would help me when I reached my destination.

The *Covenant* was bound for the United States. At this time, there was a good market for slaves on the plantations. Alas! This was the fate my wicked uncle had planned for me.

Ransome, the cabin boy, sometimes came to visit me. He worked and slept in the ship's roundhouse. Sometimes he was in pain from a wound inflicted by Mr. Shuan. It hurt my heart to see this pitiful, friendless boy. But the men respected Mr. Shuan. They said he was the only true seaman on the ship—and a good enough man when he was sober.

Mr. Riach was often kind to me. One day I swore him to secrecy, and told my whole story. He offered to help me write to both Mr. Campbell and Mr. Rankeillor. They were the ones, he said, who could help me get what was rightfully mine.

One night we heard whispering around the forecastle: "Shuan has done him in at last." We all knew who they meant. A few minutes later, Captain Hoseason came to me, and—to my surprise—spoke to me kindly.

"My man, we want you to serve in the roundhouse," he said. "You and Ransome are to change beds."

As he spoke, two sailors came by, carrying Ransome in their arms. His face was white as wax, and he wore a dreadful, fixed smile. My blood ran cold at the sight.

"Go on!" Hoseason hissed at me. "Get up to the roundhouse *now*!"

The roundhouse, where I would now sleep

and serve, was a large room. A big table was there, along with a bench and beds. All the food and drink, as well as all the weapons, were stored there, too.

When I entered, Mr. Shuan was seated at the table. A bottle of brandy and a tin cup were before him.

Mr. Riach gave the captain a glance as he came in. As plain as if he'd spoken, we knew that Ransome was dead. We looked at Mr. Shuan, who stared hard at the table.

Suddenly, in a rage, Mr. Riach took the

brandy bottle and tossed it out the window. Mr. Shuan was on his feet in a moment, a dangerous look on his face.

"Sit down!" the captain roared. "Do you know what you've done, you drunken pig? You've *murdered* the boy!"

Mr. Shuan seemed to understand. He put his hand to his head and mumbled, "Well, he brought me a dirty cup."

Captain Hoseason led him across the room to his bunk and told him to go to sleep. Mr. Shuan cried a little, but obeyed.

Mr. Riach glared at the captain. "You should have stopped him a long time ago," he snarled. "It's too late now."

"Mr. Riach, what happened tonight must never reach home," the captain said. "The boy went overboard; that's what the story is. And I would give five pounds if it were true!" Then he added, "There was no sense in throwing the bottle away, Mr. Riach. Here, David, get me another." He tossed me the key. "You'll want a glass yourself, Mr. Riach. That was an ugly thing to see."

In the following days, poor Ransome's

shadow lay on all of us. Mr. Shuan's mind was troubled. Sometimes he looked at me in confusion. "Were you here before?" he'd ask. "Was there another boy?" For all my disgust, I felt rather sorry for him.

But I had troubles of my own. Now I was doing dirty work for three men I despised. One of them, at least, should have been hung. And my future was to be a slave in the tobacco fields! Sometimes, I was even glad of the work, for it kept me from thinking.

Fighting rough seas and fierce headwinds, we had made little headway—even losing distance on some days. We were already 10 days out from Scotland's east coast—but no more than a day off its west coast. Then one night, the fog was so thick we couldn't see one end of the ship from the other. I was serving supper when the ship struck something with a great crashing noise.

It turned out that we had hit a boat—and sent her to the bottom. Only one man had survived. Somehow the fellow had leapt up and caught hold of the *Covenant*'s bow.

The captain brought the man into the roundhouse. Small and dark, he had very light eyes with a kind of dancing madness in them. I decided I would rather have him as a friend than an enemy.

The stranger spoke plainly to the captain. He said he was a Scotsman and a Jacobite. As he took a money belt from his waist, the captain stared at it, excited.

"Not one bit of this money is mine," the stranger said. "It is for my chief, who lives in exile in France. His property is in the hands of King George of England. But the poor people of Scotland send what they can to help their chief. I am their messenger. If you will take me to France, I can reward you well."

With that, the stranger and the captain made a bargain. Then the captain hurried out.

Alone with the stranger, I dared to ask, "And so you're a Jacobite?"

"Yes," he said, "And I'd guess by your long face that you're a Whig."

Whigs were the political party that was set against the Jacobites. In fact, I truly was a Whig, but I didn't wish to annoy him. "I'm betwixt and between," I said.

The stranger asked me for a drink.

When I went to get the key from the captain, he was talking to Mr. Riach. I had a feeling they were up to no good.

Noticing me, the captain said, "That Scotsman's a danger to the ship, and an enemy of our good King George. Do you see, David, what the trouble is? All our weapons are in the roundhouse—right under this man's nose! If you can bring me a pistol or two, I'll keep that in mind when we get to America. And see here: That man's belt is full of gold. For your help, I give you my word that you shall have your fingers in it."

I agreed, of course, to do as he asked. But really, I didn't know what to do. These men had stolen me from my country. And they had murdered poor Ransome. Could I stand by and watch another murder? Yet the fear of death was plain before me. What chance did I have against the entire crew?

As I went into the roundhouse, my mind was suddenly made up. I looked directly in the stranger's eyes and asked, "Do you want to be killed?"

He sprang to his feet and stared at me.

"They've murdered one boy already!" I informed him. "You're next."

The man studied my face, trying to decide if he could trust me. "They haven't got me yet," he said. "Will you stand with me?"

"I will!" I cried out.

He smiled and asked, "What's your name?"

"David Balfour," I said. And for the first time I added, "of Shaws."

He drew himself up proudly. "And *I* am Alan Breck Stewart," he said.

After we examined the weapons in the roundhouse, he handed me a cutlass. Then he set out some pistols for me to load. After that, we waited.

# 4

I Fight a Battle

Alan stood at the door, a dagger in one hand and a sword in the other. I was to guard the skylight and the other door with pistols.

We didn't have long to wait. A few minutes later, the captain came in.

Alan pointed a sword at him. "Stand!" he barked.

"A naked sword?" the captain sneered. "This it what I get for my hospitality?"

"The sooner this fight begins," Alan said, "the sooner you'll taste the steel of my sword."

The captain gave me an ugly look. "I'll remember this, David," he muttered. In the next moment, he was gone.

There was a murmur of voices outside the door. Then I heard the clash of steel, and I knew they were handing out cutlasses.

My heart beat like a bird's. I wished the thing would begin, and be over with!

It came all of a sudden. First, there was a rush of feet and a muffled roar. Then I saw Mr. Shuan just inside the doorway, crossing swords with Alan.

"He's the one who killed the boy!" I shouted at Alan.

"Watch your window!" Alan yelled. Then he ran his sword through Mr. Shuan's body.

As I turned to the window, I saw five men carrying a thick log. They intended to use it as a battering ram. I had never fired a pistol— but it was now or never. I shot at them. I must have hit someone, for a man cried out in pain. When I fired two more times, they turned and ran.

Blood was pouring from Mr. Shuan's mouth as two burly men dragged him out of the roundhouse. I believe that I watched him die while they were doing it.

Alan's sword was red with blood. He looked invincible. "They'll be back," he said.

Again, we waited. Someone dropped softly onto the roof above me. Then the skylight smashed into a thousand pieces. Several men rushed the door as another man leaped through the open skylight and landed on the floor. I held my pistol to his back. But at the touch of his live body, I could not pull the trigger. He whipped around and grabbed hold of me. I shrieked—and shot him. He gave a horrible groan and fell to the floor. Then a second man came leaping through the skylight. I shot him in the thigh, and when he fell, I shot him again.

I heard Alan shout for help. While he was fighting two men, a third man had grabbed him. Alan was stabbing at the man while still fighting off the others. My heart sank! I thought we were lost.

But the man who had grabbed Alan finally fell. With a roar, Alan charged the others. His sword flashed, and with every flash came the scream of a man hurt. In less than a minute, they were all gone.

The roundhouse was a shambles. Three men were dead, and another was dying. But Alan and I were victorious and unhurt.

"Come to my arms!" Alan cried out in triumph. "I love you like a brother, David. And, oh, man, am I not a bonny fighter?" His eyes were as bright as those of a five-year-old child with a new toy.

The thought of the two men I had shot weighed down on me. Suddenly the fight seemed like a sickening nightmare. I shuddered and began to sob.

Alan clapped a hand on my shoulder. He didn't mock my tears. I was a brave lad, he said, who only needed some sleep.

"I'll take the first watch," he offered. "You've done very well by me, David. And I wouldn't lose you for anything."

The next morning, Alan cut off a silver button from his coat. "I'm giving you this as a keepsake for last night's work," he said. "Wherever you go, if you show that button, friends of Alan Breck will help you."

He made this claim as if he had armies at his command. I admired the man's courage— but it was hard not to smile at his vanity.

A little later, Mr. Riach called to us from the deck. He pleaded with us to come out and talk. I climbed through the skylight and just sat there, a pistol in my hand.

Mr. Riach looked out of heart and very

weary. He'd been up all night, taking care of the wounded men. "The captain would like to speak to your friend," he called out to me.

"How can we trust him?" I asked. "How do we know he's not plotting something?"

"He has no plot, David," Mr. Riach tried to assure me. "And I'll tell you the honest truth. If he did, the men wouldn't go along with it. All we want is to take your friend where he's going—and see the last of him."

Soon, the captain came to one of the windows. He looked stern and pale and old. His arm was in a sling. Seeing the pistol in Alan's hand, he said, "Put that thing down!"

"Only if you set me on shore, as you promised," Alan replied.

"We are a few hours from the town of Ardnamerchan," the captain said. "I can make sure you get there—for a price."

"And let your soldiers take me?" Alan scoffed. "If you want to earn your money, set me down on the coast."

"But this part of the coast is dangerous," the captain objected. "It's a risk to the ship— and to your own lives as well."

"Take it or want it," Alan snorted.

The captain shook his head, but agreed.

Then Alan and I were left alone in the roundhouse. We smoked a pipe or two of the captain's fine tobacco. Then we listened to each other's stories. I was astonished to learn that Alan had once been in the English army.

"I was very poor," Alan explained. "That was the reason I enlisted. But I deserted—and that's a comfort to me."

Just then it occurred to me that the punishment for desertion was death. "Why do you come back to Scotland?" I asked. "You'll be put to death if you're caught!"

He gathered his thoughts. "France is a fine place," he said, "but I miss the heather and the deer. The main reason, though, is to support our chief. He's in exile in France. The people of Scotland send him whatever money they can spare. Do you see, Davie? I'm the one who carries it." He struck his belt to make the gold coins ring.

Then he told me about a man called the Red Fox. This man was an agent of King George's. When he learned that the people of

Scotland were sending money to their chief, he turned them out of their homes. "If only I can get a chance to hunt the Red Fox!" Alan cried out. "There's not enough heather in all of Scotland to hide him!"

"But this Red Fox is just following orders," I pointed out. "And if you killed him tomorrow, where would you be? They'd find another man to fill his shoes soon enough."

"You're a good lad in a fight," Alan said with a chuckle. "But, man—you have Whig blood in you!"

5 Stranded and Alone

That night, Captain Hoseason stuck his head in the roundhouse door.

"Here, man," he said to Alan. "Come out to help me pilot the ship."

"Is this one of your tricks?" Alan asked.

"Tricks!" the captain roared. "Do I look like tricks? My ship's in danger!"

He sounded truly worried. We nodded at each other and stepped onto the deck.

Alan looked out and saw that the sea was breaking on reefs. "I'm thinking these might be the Torran Rocks," he said.

The captain frowned. "And how far do they go?" he asked nervously.

"Well, I'm not a pilot," Alan said, "but I've heard they go on for ten miles."

The captain and Mr. Riach looked at each other. Their faces were grim.

As we sailed on, more and more reefs

loomed ahead. The night was bright, and we could see them clearly. Before long the ship was dangerously close to the reefs. Yet through it all, Mr. Riach and the captain were as steady as steel. They had not done very well in the fighting. But now I saw that they were brave in their own trade.

I noticed that Alan's face was white with fear. "David," he said quietly, "this is not the kind of death I want."

"What, Alan!" I cried out. "Surely you're not *afraid*?"

"Not really," he said quickly, "but you'll admit it would be a sad, cold ending."

A few minutes later, Mr. Riach spotted clear water ahead. We were headed for it, when all at once, the tide caught the ship and threw the wind out of her sails. Then she came around into the wind like a top. The next moment, she hit the reef so hard we were thrown flat on the deck.

As the high waves broke over us, we could feel the poor *Covenant* being ground to pieces against the reef!

Preparing to escape, some sailors were

helping Mr. Riach pull out a boat. Even the wounded men were trying to help. The captain did nothing. He was mumbling to himself and groaning whenever his ship hammered down on the rocks.

At last we had the boat ready to launch. Some wounded men—those who couldn't move—screamed out for us to save them.

Suddenly, one of the sailors yelled, "*Hold on!*" in a shrill voice. A moment later a huge wave broke over us. It lifted the whole ship up so sharply that I was thrown overboard.

I went under and came up, again and again. Waves pushed me forward, then beat down on me. Then, all of a sudden, the water around me was calm.

Looking around, I was amazed at how far I was from the ship! I yelled—but I knew the *Covenant* was too far away. I couldn't tell if they'd launched the boat or not.

The shore glimmered in the moonlight. I had no skill in swimming, but after an hour of kicking and splashing, I managed to reach land.

When my feet touched earth, the unhappiest part of my adventure was only beginning. The night was very cold. I passed some time walking back and forth, beating my chest to keep warm.

As soon as day broke, I climbed a rocky hill and looked out. No ship or boat was in sight. I felt sad and lonely, and my belly rumbled with hunger. I'd hoped the sun would rise and dry my wet clothes, but it started to rain. What could I do? I set off toward the east, hoping to find a house.

Instead, I discovered a creek that separated me from the mainland. I was on a rocky little island! I tried to cross the creek, but the water was deep, and moving too quickly. Finally, I dropped down on the sand and wept.

The time I spent on the island is still a horrible memory. I will pass over it quickly.

To satisfy my hunger, I tried eating raw shellfish. At first, they tasted wonderful. But as soon as I had eaten, I got terribly sick. But later, I was so hungry I ate them again. This time I was all right. I never knew what to expect on the island. Sometimes I was miserably sick and sometimes not. I never knew which kind of shellfish sickened me.

All day, it rained. There wasn't a dry spot to be found! That night, I lay down with my head between two rocks, my feet in a puddle.

The next day, I walked to every side of the island. But I found nothing except rocks and heather, and a few birds.

Climbing up a little hillside, I could see smoke rising from houses in the distance. It made me yearn for warm fires and company, and my heart ached.

Another day passed. I kept watch for boats passing by, but saw none.

By the next day, my wet clothes were beginning to rot. My throat was sore, and I was weak. I could hardly bear to look at shellfish, knowing that was all I had to eat.

Yet the worst was yet to come.

I was looking out to sea when I spotted two fishermen in a boat. They were so close I could see the color of their hair. I shouted out to them. They looked around, said some Gaelic words to each other—and laughed. The boat kept on going.

I couldn't believe such wickedness! I ran from rock to rock, crying out to them frantically. I thought my heart would burst, but they kept on rowing away.

The next day, the boat came by again. This time, a third man was with them. He stood up in the boat and called to me. I could only make out a few words, but I did catch the word "tide." The man kept waving his hand toward the mainland.

"You mean when the tide is out—" I cried.

"Yes, yes!" he answered. "*Tide.*"

They began to laugh. I turned away from them and ran toward the creek. By now it had shrunk to a trickle, hardly above my knees. I dashed through the water, and landed with a shout on the mainland.

In the course of my life, I've seen many wicked men and fools. I believe that both are paid in the end—but the fools first.

I walked toward the smoke I'd seen so often. At last, I came to a small house where a man sat, smoking a pipe. He spoke little English. But he was able to tell me that several men had been there the day before. And one of them was Alan!

"I know who you are. You must be the lad

with the silver coat button!" he said.

He gave me a message: Alan said he'd wait to meet me in the town of Torosay.

The kind man and his wife gave me supper. Although I offered money, he would accept nothing for his generosity.

The next day I set out for Torosay. The Highland people I met along the way seemed very poor. There were beggars everywhere.

Many of the Highlanders were dressed strangely. Their traditional plaid kilts had been forbidden by the English. So, since kilts were outlawed, they mocked the law. Some men wore no pants at all, but only a coat. Some carried their pants on their backs!

I walked until night, when I came to a lone house. There, a man agreed to let me stay the night, if I would pay him. He promised to guide me to Torosay the following day.

The next morning we'd barely started out when he demanded more money. I gave him a little more. But after a few miles, he sat down and took off his shoes. He said he would go no further. I was angry now, and raised my hand to strike him.

At that, he drew a knife and sat grinning at me. But I was a strong lad, and very angry. I ran at him, grabbed the knife with one hand, and hit him with the other. Taking his knife and shoes, I went on down the road.

About an hour later, I met a great, ragged, blind fellow with a cane. He told me he was a religious teacher, but his face looked dark and dangerous. As we walked along, I saw the butt of a pistol sticking out from his coat.

He said he would guide me to Torosay for a drink of brandy. Then he started to question me, asking if I was rich. As we went on, he walked closer and closer to me.

Finally, I told him that I had a pistol, too. I warned him to get away from me or I would blow his brains out.

That night, I stayed at an inn. The innkeeper told me about the blind man. "He's a very dangerous fellow," he said. "He can shoot by the ear at several yards. And he's been accused of murder as well as robbery. You were lucky to get away from him!"

# 6 Witness to Murder

The next day, I took a ferry from Torosay to the mainland. On board, I learned that the ferry's skipper was Neil Roy Macrob—and that he belonged to Alan's clan. I was anxious to speak with Neil Roy alone.

Both passengers and crew sang as they rowed together. It was a pretty thing to see. Then we saw a large ship, crowded with people. As we drew past it, we heard weeping and wailing. The ship's passengers cried out to those on shore. Then I understood: It was an emigrant ship, leaving home for America.

Finally, I was able to talk to Neil Roy. "I'm looking for Alan Breck Stewart," I said quietly. Then, foolishly, I tried to give him some money.

The offer of money truly offended the man. "You should *never* offer your dirty money to a Highland gentleman," he said.

"And you should never say Alan Breck's name aloud to anyone."

I tried to apologize, but it was difficult. I had no idea that the fellow was a gentleman.

When I showed him my silver button, he told me where I could find Alan. I was to go to Aucharn, he said, and stay there with James of the Glens.

Early on the next day's journey, I met a small, stout man named Henderland. He was a religious teacher, but very unlike the blind man I had met before. This fellow seemed to be moderate in his politics, so I asked him about the Red Fox.

"It's a bad business, what this Red Fox is doing," he said. "It's a wonder that the poor people *have* any money to send their chief. They're nearly starving! But they do look up to their leaders. There's James of the Glens. He's the half-brother of the chief. And then there's the one they call Alan Breck—"

"And what of him?" I asked.

"Ha! What of the wind that blows?" he answered. "He's here and then he's gone. For all we can tell, he could be watching us from behind a bush right now. We'd never know it. But this Red Fox, the king's agent—he's putting his head in a bee's nest."

"I heard he's coming here to turn the people out of their homes," I said. "Do you think they'll fight back?"

"They're disarmed, or supposed to be," he said. "But I expect there's still a good many weapons tucked away in quiet places."

The next day I set out again. I was in a steep wooded area when I heard the sound of horses. Four men came up the road. The first was a red-headed gentleman. The second, wearing black clothes and white wig, looked like a lawyer. The third was a servant, and the fourth was a sheriff's officer. I learned later that many red-coated English soldiers were marching at some distance behind them.

As they drew near, I greeted them and asked the way to Aucharn.

"The Red Fox wants to know who you're looking for," the servant replied. Aha! The red-headed man was indeed the Red Fox.

"James of the Glens," I said.

The Red Fox turned to the lawyer. "Do

you think James of the Glens is gathering his people?"

Before the lawyer could answer, we all heard a gunshot. The Red Fox fell from his horse.

"Oh, I am dead!" he cried out.

The lawyer jumped from his horse and held him. But the Red Fox's head rolled on his shoulders, and he passed away.

I ran up a nearby hill to see if I could catch sight of the murderer. I glimpsed a big man in a black coat, with a long rifle.

"Here!" I cried to the others. "I see him!"

I began to run after him, but a soft voice called me back. When I looked down I saw the lawyer and the sheriff's officer were below me. Soldiers were rushing up to them.

"Ten pounds if you catch the lad!" the lawyer cried. "That boy must surely be an accomplice. He was posted here to stop us, so the murderer could take aim."

A new terror filled me.

"Duck in here," the voice whispered.

Hidden among the trees stood Alan Breck, holding a fishing rod. "Come!" he said.

We ran and ducked through the woods. Finally, when I was certain my heart would surely burst, we stopped to rest.

After I could breathe again, I said, "You and I must go our separate ways. I like you a lot, Alan. But murder is not my way."

Alan laid his dagger out on his hand. "I swear by this iron that I had no part in this murder," he said solemnly.

"Thanks be for that!" I said, offering him my hand. "Do you know who did it? Did you recognize that man in the black coat?"

"He may have been near me," Alan said, "but I think I was tying my shoes just then."

What kind of an answer was that? "Can you swear that you don't know him?" I demanded.

"Not yet—but I have a great memory for forgetting, David," he said.

"There's one thing I saw clearly," I went on. "You exposed yourself—as well as me—so the murderer could get away."

"Perhaps that's true," Alan admitted, "and so would any gentleman."

Half-laughing, half-angry at Alan, I gave up. He looked so innocent! And the man was clearly ready to sacrifice himself for what he believed. So I kept quiet.

After a few minutes, Alan said we must be on our way again. He pointed out that I was in danger as well as he.

"But I've done no wrong," I insisted. "I'm not afraid of justice."

"You don't understand," he said. "The Red Fox was a Campbell. You'd be tried in the Campbells' main town. And there would be fifteen Campbells on the jury."

This frightened me a little, I admit.

"We're in the Highlands," Alan went on. "When I tell you to run, Davie, take my word for it and *run*. It's hard to run and starve in the heather. But it's harder still to lie chained in a redcoat prison!"

7 | On the Run with Alan

We struck out for Aucharn. There, James of the Glens would give us food and money. On the way, Alan told me what had finally happened to the *Covenant*, and her men.

As the ship was sinking on the reef, the crew had finally got the boat into the water. Just as they reached shore, Captain Hoseason had turned on Alan. In spite of his promise, he'd even ordered the men to attack him!

"But the men were reluctant," Alan said. "Mr. Riach held them back and told me to run for it. This seemed like very good advice, and I took it."

That night we reached the house of James of the Glens. As we approached, Alan gave three whistles as a password.

We were greeted by a tall, handsome man of about 50. This was James. Nervously wringing his hands, he said, "The death of the

Red Fox will bring trouble for all of us! And I am a man with a family!"

I noticed James's servants hurrying about. Some were lifting thatch from the roof of the house. From under the thatch, they pulled out guns, swords, and other weapons. I could see their faces by the light of the torches they carried. They were full of panic.

James gave each of us a sword, a pistol, and a few small coins. His wife made up a packet containing some oatmeal, a pan, and a bottle of brandy. One of James's sons gave me a change of clothes.

Then we were off again, leaving that house of fear behind.

All night long we walked and ran and walked and ran. When day came, we were in a great valley that had a foaming river cutting through it.

"This is no good," Alan said. "It's a place they're bound to watch."

We moved downriver to where the water was split by three rocks. Alan didn't hesitate. He jumped clean onto the middle rock, quickly squatting to get his balance. The rock was very small indeed. He could easily have toppled over into the fast-paced current.

I took a deep breath. Before I could think twice, I jumped to his side—and he caught me!

There we stood, teetering on a slippery rock. The next jump was a far greater distance. A deadly feeling of sickness and fear came over me. I put my hand over my eyes.

Alan shook me. Then he forced the brandy bottle between my lips and made me drink. "Hang or drown!" he shouted as he leaped across and landed safely.

I knew that if I didn't leap at once, I would never leap at all. Trying not to think about it, I bent low, then flung myself forward. My hands reached the far bank, but then slipped. Alan seized me, first by the hair, then by the collar. With a great effort, he pulled me ashore.

After a short rest, we set off again, running for our lives. I was tired and bruised, hoping he'd slow down soon.

Alan stopped beneath two great rocks standing close together. Both were about 20 feet high. After scrambling up to the top, he took off his belt and dangled it over the side.

I held it tightly, and he hauled me up.

At the top, the two rocks combined to form a kind of large bowl. As many as three or four men could have hidden there! Alan took the first watch, and let me sleep. When I woke, it was midday and very hot. We could see the redcoats' camp about a mile away. Dozens of sentries were on patrol.

The sun beat down on us cruelly. After a while, the rocks grew so hot we could hardly touch them. We had only raw brandy to drink, which was worse than nothing.

About two o'clock, we could stand it no longer. There was a bit of shade on one side of the rock. We dropped down and rested there. Unfortunately, we were in full view of any redcoat who might pass by. But none came. Finally, little by little, we crept away to a stream.

Hidden by the bank, we drank again and again, and bathed as well as we could.

When night fell, we set forth again. Leaving the valley, we began to climb up the mountainside itself.

Early the next day, we reached our

destination. This was a small cave high on the mountainside. In this snug hideout we lived quite happily for five days.

Then Alan decided he should send word to James of the Glens. We needed more money.

I had no idea how he could contact the fellow. But Alan was a clever man. From the ashes of our fire, he took two sticks of wood. Then he tore strips from his coat, covered the sticks, and bound them together in a cross. A burning cross, he explained, was a sign of his clan. Next, he asked to borrow the button he had given me. Then he attached the button, along with sprigs of pine and birch, to the cross.

"My good friend, John Breck Maccoll, lives nearby," Alan said. "Tonight, I will stick the cross in his window. John Breck cannot read—but the cross will tell him that I'm hiding in a place where both birch and pine grow. He will know to look up here in the cave."

It worked! The next day we had a visit from John Breck. Alan told him to tell James of the Glens that we needed more money.

When he returned three days later, John brought a little money from James's wife—and bad news. James was in prison. He and some of his servants were suspected of helping the Red Fox's murderers to escape. The rumor was that Alan himself had fired the shot. A hundred-pound reward had been offered for the capture of the two of us!

8 Hiding in the Highlands

The next day, Alan and I traveled hard and fast. Just as John had warned, we spotted the redcoats searching for us.

After many hours, we lay down at last to rest. Alan took the first watch. It seemed as if I had just closed my eyes when he shook me awake to take my turn.

We had no clock. But Alan stuck a sprig of heather in the ground. As soon as the heather's shadow moved to the east, I was to wake him. But I fell asleep. When I woke, I nearly cried out loud, for it was very late. In the distance, I could see a full company of redcoats, searching the land.

I woke Alan, and quickly confessed what I had done. He gave me a sharp look, both ugly and anxious. "It's death to go back the way we came," he said. "We have to go around them. So come now, David, be quick!"

We wound in and out of the heather. Sometimes we hid behind a big bush, caught our breath, and looked out at the soldiers.

My body was weak and aching. Nothing but fear of Alan kept me going. The man's face was red, blotched with patches of white. His breath whistled as it came. But nothing seemed to dash his spirits.

Finally, I told him I could go no farther.

Alan looked at me with steady eyes. Then he simply said, "I'll carry you."

I stared at him. The little man was dead serious. The sight of so much determination shamed me deeply.

"Lead away!" I said. "I'll follow."

With the coming of night, it grew cooler and darker. But at last, we were out of the greatest danger. Now that we were able to stand up again, we stumbled along like dead folk. So stupid from weariness were we that we fell into an ambush!

First, the bushes around us began to rustle. Then several ragged men sprang out at us. The next moment, we were on our backs, their daggers at our throats!

I lay there for a moment, too tired to be afraid. Then Alan spoke to them in Gaelic—and the daggers were put away! Soon we were all sitting together.

"Ah, we're in luck, Davie! These men are Cluny's sentries," Alan explained.

Tired as I was, I came awake from surprise. "Cluny!" I cried. "Is he still here?" I knew that Cluny Macpherson had a price on his head. I'd heard that he was living in France.

"He's still here—in spite of King George," Alan answered proudly.

We went to see Cluny. As we walked along with the sentries, a dreadful lightness came over me. I had trouble walking. Alan looked at me, frowning. A minute later, two sentries grabbed my arms and carried me along.

We went up, up, into the heart of the mountain called Ben Alder. At last we reached Cluny's place, an egg-shaped house with a tree at the center. The walls were made of poles and moss. We were told that the countryfolk called it "Cluny's Cage." It was one of many places that Cluny used as hideouts.

We learned that he sometimes had visitors.

At night, his wife or close friends might come to see him. And every morning, a barber arrived to bring him news and shave him. Even though King George had made him an outlaw, Cluny was still a leader to his people. As such, he settled disputes among them, and they greeted him like a king.

After we ate and drank, a strange heaviness came over me. I lay down and fell into a kind of trance. Sometimes I was awake, and could see what was happening. At other times I could only hear voices.

There was a doctor who visited me. He spoke only Gaelic, so I couldn't understand him. All I knew was that I was ill. As I tossed about in a fever, Alan and Cluny played cards.

The next day, Alan asked me to loan him my money. My father had warned me against gambling, but I was too sick to refuse.

Soon all of my money—along with Alan's and Cluny's—was moving back and forth across the table. They played on and on.

On the third day, I woke up very weak, but the fever had passed. It was then I noticed that there was no money on the table. Alan had a guilty, embarrassed look on his face.

"The little money we have must carry us a long way," I reminded him.

He looked at the ground before saying, "David, I've lost it. That's the naked truth."

"*My* money, too?" I howled.

"Your money, too," Alan admitted with a groan. "You shouldn't have given it to me, David. I'm an idiot when I play cards."

"Hoot-toot!" Cluny cried. "You shall have your money back! I would not hinder men in your situation!" Then he pulled some gold from his pocket and laid it before me.

I felt like a beggar, but I thanked him. Then I took stock of myself. I was weak, but well enough to walk. That afternoon, Alan and I started off again.

I was angry at Alan for behaving like a child. For hours I wouldn't look him in the eye, or speak to him. I knew that he was ashamed and I was behaving badly, but I was angry at myself as well.

It was a dreadful time. I was never warm. I had a sore throat and a painful stitch in my side. When we slept, with the rain beating down on us, I remembered the worst of my adventures: the tower of Shaws lit up by lightning; poor Ransome being carried out by sailors; Shuan dead on the roundhouse floor; the Red Fox dying before me.

On the third day of our journey, Alan looked at me, concerned. He offered to carry my pack. I refused, coldly.

Then Alan began to tease. The kindest thing he called me was "Whig." I knew that my stubborn silence had caused the teasing.

All the while, my health was growing worse and worse. Flushes of heat would come over me, then spasms of shivering. Suddenly, I was ready to have it out with Alan. I cruelly insulted his family, the Stewarts.

When he yelped in anger, I drew my sword.

"David!" Alan cried. "Are you daft? I can't fight you! It would be murder!" He too had automatically drawn his sword, but now he threw it to the ground. "I *cannot*!"

At this, all the anger oozed out of me. I realized then that no apology could ever blot out my insults. But a cry for help might very well draw Alan to my side.

"Alan!" I wailed. "If you cannot help me, I must die here. I can't breathe right. My legs are fainting under me. If I die, will you forgive me? In my heart I always liked you— even when I was angriest."

"David, man!" Alan was close to sobbing. "Here, lean on me. We'll find a house and you can rest." Then he put his arm around me and gently led me forward.

"I've got neither sense nor kindness," he went on. "I forgot you were hardly more than a child. Why couldn't I see that you were dying on your feet? Davie, *you* will have to try to forgive *me*!"

"Alan," I cried, "what makes you so good to me? How can you be so kind to such an ungrateful fellow?"

"I don't know," Alan replied. "What I thought I liked best about you was that you never quarreled with me. And now I like you even better!"

9 Meeting Mr. Rankeillor

Alan knocked at the door of the first house we reached. This was a dangerous thing to do, but luck was with us. The house belonged to the Maclarens. Alan was welcome there, both for his name and his reputation.

The family sent for a doctor, who said I was very ill indeed. I was in bed for more than a week. And it was a month before I was fit to travel again.

During those weeks, the Maclarens had another guest, Robin Oig. He was a son of the notorious Rob Roy. When Robin and Alan met, they looked at each other like strange dogs. Insults were exchanged. Clearly, the feud between their families was an old one. After just a few minutes, they were about to draw swords.

Just then, Mr. Maclaren spoke up. "Gentlemen!" he said. "Both of you have a reputation for playing the pipes. Which of you is best is an old dispute. Now, we have a good chance to settle it."

The old man hurried to fetch his pipes. Robin went first, playing a merry little tune. Then Alan took the pipes and played the same tune—but he added variations.

When Robin played again, he copied Alan's variations perfectly. Then he revised them anew. I was amazed to hear him.

Alan's face grew dark and hot. Then Robin played a piece that was a favorite of the Stewarts. I could see Alan's anger die out as he thought only of the music. At last, he declared Robin a great piper. Both men played through the night, and the quarrel was made up.

When I was well, Alan and I set out again. We'd almost run out of money. If I didn't reach Mr. Rankeillor soon—or if he refused to help me—we would surely starve.

Luckily, the month was August, and the weather was beautiful and warm. Alan thought that the redcoats' hunt for us had slackened.

After an easy journey, we came to the river

Forth. As soon as we crossed the river, I would be safe. The night was dark, so I wanted to go straight across the bridge. But Alan was wary.

"It seems awfully quiet," he said in a low voice. "Let's wait just a bit, and be sure."

As we waited, an old woman crossed the bridge. It was too dark to see, but we heard a musket rattle. "Who goes?" a voice called out. It was a sentry.

"This will not do, David," Alan whispered.

"Oh, man, it breaks my heart!" I sighed. Mr. Rankeillor was on the south shore—wealth was waiting for me there. But here I was on the north, with only pennies to my name. Worse yet, I was dressed in dirty clothes, and I had a price on my head. And my only friend was an outlaw!

At a public house, we bought bread and cheese from a pretty lass. We ate outside, by the water. There, Alan formed a plan.

He half-carried me back inside and asked the lass for brandy. Then he fed me bits of bread and cheese, as if I were a child. His face was full of worry as he told the lass I was sick and tired to death from wandering in the hills.

The girl was sympathetic. "Poor lamb!" she cooed. Then she brought us more food to eat.

Next Alan hinted that I was a Jacobite, with a price on my head. He said that only a boat would save me from the hangman's noose. He asked for her help.

The lass seemed troubled, as if she weren't sure what to do. Deciding to tell her a little of the truth, I said I was on my way to see Mr. Rankeillor. Although there was a price on my head, I said that it was because of an accident. King George had no truer friend than I.

Her face cleared at this, although Alan's darkened.

"I know of Mr. Rankeillor," she said. "He's a good man. Trust me—I'll find some way to get you across the river."

We shook her hand and went to wait in the woods. About eleven that night, we heard the splash of oars. It was the lass herself! She'd stolen the neighbor's boat and come for us. I tried to thank her, but she touched my lips, warning me to be silent.

Even after she was gone, we said little to each other. Indeed, there were no words to acknowledge such a great kindness.

Queensferry, where Mr. Rankeillor lived, was an easy night's journey. We agreed that Alan would fend for himself until sunset. Then we would meet in a nearby field.

I was in the long street of Queensferry before the sun came up. Fear gripped me, for I had no real proof of who I was. And I was ashamed of my tattered clothes. Asking for directions, I finally stopped before a fine-looking house. Then it happened that an important-looking man stepped out. He asked me what I was doing.

I told him my name and said I was looking for Mr. Rankeillor.

He was surprised. "I am that man," he said, and he invited me to step inside.

In a great rush of words, I told him I'd been kidnapped by Captain Hoseason. Then I described the shipwreck on the reefs.

"That matches pretty well with the information I have," he said. "Several months ago, your friend Mr. Campbell came to my office. He demanded to know what had happened to you. Of course, I'd never known of your existence—but I knew your father. So I questioned Mr. Ebenezer. He said that he'd given you a great sum of money—which seemed improbable. According to him, you'd gone to Europe to finish your education. But Mr. Campbell wasn't satisfied with that story. After all, he'd never heard from you.

"Then we heard from Mr. Hoseason," Mr. Rankeillor went on. "He said you'd drowned in the shipwreck. That was in June, but now it's August. That's a gap of two full months. Tell me what happened."

I told him my story, from the beginning. When I mentioned Alan Breck's name, Mr. Rankeillor stopped me. "You'd better not use any Highland names," he said. "If you please, call your friend Mr. Thompson."

When I'd finally finished my story, Mr. Rankeillor smiled. "Mr. David," he said, "I believe you're near the end of your troubles!"

§10 I Claim My Inheritance

Mr. Rankeillor then told me a great deal about my father, Alexander, and his brother Ebenezer. When he was young, Ebenezer had been a gallant man. Then he and Alexander had fallen in love with the same woman. Ebenezer was sure that he would win her— but she had refused him.

"He couldn't accept that his brother had gotten the best of him," Mr. Rankeillor went on. "Ebenezer screamed like a peacock. The whole country heard about it!"

Finally, the Balfour brothers struck an odd bargain: Alexander would keep the lady, and Ebenezer would keep the estate.

As people heard the story, they gave Ebenezer the cold shoulder for being spoiled and weak. When Alexander disappeared, there was even talk of murder! No one knew the young couple had moved away to live and die as poor folk. But after that, everyone avoided Ebenezer.

"Well, sir," I asked, "what is my position?"

"The estate is yours," Mr. Rankeillor said. "But it will be quite difficult to prove. Your uncle will fight you, certainly. And lawsuits are often very expensive."

As he was talking, I'd been forming a plan. I explained it to Mr. Rankeillor.

After thinking it over, he agreed to it. A few minutes later we set off, along with his servant, Torrance, to find Alan.

Alan was ready and eager when I told him about the part he would play. To protect Alan, Mr. Rankeillor told him he'd forgotten his glasses. His vision was so poor, Mr. Rankeillor went on, that he was sure to forget what Alan looked like.

It was dark by the time we reached the house of Shaws. Just as we'd planned, Mr. Rankeillor, Torrance, and I waited outside by the corner of the house. Alan went to the door and knocked.

After some time, my uncle opened the window, blunderbuss in hand. "What brings

me here is David," Alan announced.

Ebenezer came to the door. "Huh! I'd better let you in then," he grumbled.

But Alan insisted on talking at the doorstep. He said that a gentleman of his family had been looking for driftwood on the shore. There, he'd discovered a half-drowned boy and taken him to an old, ruined castle. The lad was still staying there, Alan went on, at great expense to his family.

"Now, what would you pay to have the boy returned?" Alan asked.

"I take no interest in the lad," my uncle snorted. "I'll pay no ransom."

"I'll put it plainly, then," Alan replied. "Do you want the lad kept, or do you want him killed?"

"Oh, *kept*!" my uncle cried. "We'll have no bloodshed, if you please. I won't have him killed by wild Highlanders."

"Very well then," Alan said. "Now, let's discuss the price. I want to know what you paid Hoseason for having him kidnapped."

"*Kidnapped!* That's a black lie!" my uncle snapped. "He was never kidnapped."

"But Hoseason himself told me that," Alan went on. "We're partners. Now I ask you again: How much did you pay him?"

"What has he told you?" my uncle asked.

"That's my business," Alan said bluntly.

"Well," Ebenezer admitted, "the truth is I did give him twenty pounds. But he had the best of the bargain. He was planning to make even more money by selling the lad in the Carolinas."

Just then, Mr. Rankeillor walked up to the doorstep. "Thank you, Mr. Thompson. That will do. Good evening, Mr. Balfour," he said.

At that point, I also stepped forward. "Good evening, Uncle Ebenezer," I said politely.

My uncle had not a word to say. He stared at us, as if he'd turned to stone.

Alan removed the blunderbuss from Ebenezer's hands. Then Mr. Rankeillor took my uncle by the arm, and led him into the house.

Torrance had brought supper in a basket. He and Alan and I sat down in the kitchen and ate. Meanwhile, my uncle and Mr. Rankeillor came to an agreement: My uncle could keep the house and land as long as he lived. But he would begin at once to pay me two-thirds of the estate's income.

For many weeks I had slept on dirt and stones. My belly was often empty, and the fear of death never left me. But tonight I lay down by the warm fire in the kitchen. Now I was a man with money and a well-respected name in the country. I could not sleep. Until dawn, I watched the flickering of the fire and planned my future.

The next day, Mr. Rankeillor advised me to hire legal help for Alan. He suggested that I find a lawyer named Stewart. Someone in his clan would surely help Alan to find a ship so he could safely get away.

The next day, Alan and I walked toward Edinburgh. He had the address of a lawyer, and I was headed for a bank in town.

We walked slowly, knowing it would soon be time to part. We tried to be merry. I joked about Mr. Rankeillor calling him "Mr. Thompson." And Alan teased me about the expensive new clothes I'd soon be wearing. But both of us were closer to tears than laughter.

We reached a spot above Edinburgh. There I gave Alan what money I had (given to me by Mr. Rankeillor). The time had come. We shook hands and said goodbye.

I dared not take one glance back at the friend I was leaving. And as I went on to Edinburgh, I felt terribly lost and lonesome. I wanted to cry like a baby.

As I entered the city, I let the crowd carry me to and fro. I looked at the huge buildings and the rows and rows of shops. I took in the constant hubbub, the foul smells, and the fine clothes. All the while, I thought of Alan.

Then luck brought me to the very door of the bank. I hoped with all my heart that luck was with Alan, too.